SLEEP TRAINING

by
Eluned Gramich

THE
Ghastling

The Ghastling Press
10 Park Street
Maesteg
Mid Glamorgan
CF34 9BA
www.theghastling.com

ISBN: 978-1-8381891-3-6

The publisher acknowledges the financial assistance of the Books Council of Wales

© Eluned Gramich 2021

The right of Eluned Gramich to be identified as the author of this work has been asserted in accordance with the Copyright, Designs and Patents Act, 1988

All rights reserved. No part of this publication may be reproduced, stored in a retrieval system, or transmitted at any time or by any means, electronic, mechanical, photocopying, recording or otherwise without the prior permission of the publisher.

This novella is entirely a work of fiction. The names, characters and incidents portrayed in it are the work of the author's imagination. Any resemblance to actual persons, living or dead, events or localities, is entirely coincidental.

A CIP catalogue record of this book is available from the British Library.
Printed by Ingram Spark, Milton Keynes
Cover design by Rhys Owain Williams

'Deep, visceral terror resides within this story. Gramich accumulates unnerving detail to build to an horrific climax. A deeply unsettling and innovative update on the classic ghost story.'

Lucie McKnight Hardy

*

'Set against the claustrophobic backdrop of the pandemic, *Sleep Training* is an unsettling mediation on new motherhood, perception, and selfhood. It is at once frightening and thoughtful, eerie and compelling, and leaves the reader questioning who and what can be trusted.'

Rebecca F. John

*

'From this novella's opening scene of exhaustion tainting the young parents' arrival at their new home, there's a creeping sense of wrongness that could just be dismissed as sleep deprivation or paranoia. The final horrors – no longer inside the mind, now inside the room – cut the reader as sharply as a wielded knife.'

Carly Holmes

To Renato

It was early March when they moved into their first house: a place Elin hadn't yet seen for herself. She was nervous on the drive down – five hours, it took, on the A-roads. She spent it clutching the car door and craning her neck to check on the baby, which irritated her husband. Mark had done the house viewing and persuaded Elin that it was a great buy. He put an offer in sharpish. Elin had agreed. She didn't know about house-buying (or 'conveyancing' as her husband called it); the expensive lawyers, the removal company, the mortgage – she was happy for Mark to do all that. She had enough work with the baby. Her mind was constantly turning on the relentless and infinite number of tasks she needed to accomplish in order to keep Padarn clean, happy, alive. There was no space for any other considerations. Apart from, now, the heavy sadness of having to leave her home town, her family and friends, for the outskirts of a city she didn't know.

When they pulled into the street, she was relieved. The place was exactly as Mark had described: terraced brick houses with neat little strips of front lawn and a longer, narrow strip of garden at the back. The new house was no different from the rest. She was relieved, because her husband, though she loved him, had a habit of understating things to make life easier for himself. Nothing too bad – halving the price of some concert tickets he'd bought so as not to alarm her, saying he'd had a pint when really, he'd had five… But the house: the house was fine. More than fine. Three bedrooms: a spare and master bedroom overlooked the garden and the third, smaller room, which would be the nursery, overlooked the street. Downstairs, there was a newly installed kitchen, a cramped dining room, and a 'good size' living room, just as Mark had promised. The carpets were grey. The walls white. The property developer had made the whole house appear as bland and clean as possible, which was alright with her.

Elin couldn't have coped with a run-down place. Even a dripping tap could cause her to break down in tears these days.

"This is nice," she said when they set foot in the grey-white living room. The baby was asleep. She unclipped the harness as carefully as possible so as not to wake him. Mark said nothing. She felt his tiredness and stress as if it were her own: the way he jangled the car keys, pushed his hair back and massaged his forehead. Mark hated driving.

Still, Elin asked, "When are the removal people going to be here? We need to get the fridge going."

"Jesus Christ. Is that really the only thing you're going to say? Our first house together and it's where's the fridge?"

"Sorry. I said it looked nice. Maybe you didn't hear me."

He turned away from her as though to go back out the front door. "Nice. Yeah, okay."

"Seriously, Mark."

Their son opened his eyes and began to whimper. Elin picked him up quickly to stop the whimpering from developing into a storm, then gave Mark a conciliatory kiss. "It looks great. Really lovely. Thank you." Her husband softened, a smile in return for the kiss. "Fancy giving us the full tour, then? Might have to be quick though. He'll be hungry soon."

"Sure."

The removal men came early in the evening when the light was waning. An orange-red sunset adorned the white walls by the time the men left. They didn't have many things, Elin and Mark, yet the boxes seemed numberless, piled up in the empty rooms after a long day. She sat on the floor with her little boy, Padarn, clamped to her breast for what felt like hours. He was too old, she thought, to feed like this, but it seemed the long journey and new surroundings had disturbed him enough to seek comfort from her body. Without a fridge, she couldn't store any

3

bottles for the night, and the prospect of missing a full night's sleep exhausted her further. Mark was in good spirits, however; he'd enjoyed talking to the removal men, directing them to the right room, offering them a beer from the warm cans he'd brought from a garage on the way. After they turned him down and left, he drank them himself.

Padarn was sleeping in Elin's arms, a small, fat hand on her collarbone, his breath hot and steady.

Mark opened his second can, took a satisfied swig. "We did it."

"Yeah." She smiled, laid her head on his shoulder. "Well done, cariad. It's beautiful here."

"Let's hope the job is just as good, isn't it."

"I'm sure it will be. It's perfect for you."

"Yeah, but people can be dicks."

"They won't be. Anyway, everybody likes you."

"Do they?"

"Of course!"

"Well, you're the only person that matters. I don't care about anybody else. You and Pads. What a chubster!"

"Yeah, he is a bit, isn't he?"

"It's because he doesn't do anything. Doesn't want to crawl or stand up."

"He's a lazy-bones."

"Yeah, like his Mum."

"Oi!" She hit him.

"Only kidding. Or am I?"

"Watch it."

He smelled nice, even though his shirt was still damp with sweat. Mark always smelled nice to her – earthy and tender. He pulled her closer to his chest, so they were all three cwtching up on the sofa, like a real little family.

*

Over the next few days, Padarn slept in the travel cot in their bedroom. Mark's job had already started in town, and so he hadn't got round to putting together the wooden one they had, which lay in pieces at the foot of the stairs. But there was another reason too. Little Padarn wasn't settling as well as usual at night. He grew irritated quickly, dispensed with a toy as soon as Elin handed him one, cried when she left the room. It was to be expected, with the move and everything.

Elin didn't mind these irritable phases because they rarely lasted more than three or four days. So she did as much unpacking as she could in the hour or two afforded to her by a nap, leaving Padarn to blabber and play in the high-chair after lunch so she could quickly stuff another box's contents into the kitchen cupboards. The work was oddly satisfying and distracting. In the old flat in west Wales, whole days and weeks would pass when she felt as though she'd done nothing, accomplished nothing. But with unpacking, every day had its little coup: the wedding cutlery in the drawer, the DVDs they owned but never watched stacked neatly on the top shelf of a bookcase. Because of the state of the kitchen, they ordered take-away every day for the first week or so; another chore struck off the list. They ordered from every local place, ranking them from best to inedible, keeping the leaflets as proof that they actually lived here now. Mark came home from his new job happy. He told her stories about his work colleagues, the funny habits they had, the way the boss once singled him out for praise at a weekly meeting.

"That's brilliant," she said, cutting Padarn's toast into finger-friendly strips. "You're doing brilliantly."

"And we have proper money coming in now," he said, hanging his jacket on the back of the kitchen chair. "Plus, who knows? In a year or two, I could get promoted."

Padarn squealed, threw one of the strips onto the floor,

another in her face.

"Fantastic, cariad. So good."

"Are you listening?"

"Yeah! Of course, bach. Sorry."

"That's okay," Mark said, picking up the toast from the floor. "Hey, mate. You being naughty? You bothering Mammy?"

"He's been a right troublemaker today."

"Has he now?"

Mark tickled him. Padarn squealed again in joy. It was sweet to see them together, father and son, but it sometimes dismayed her, too, the way Mark could so easily win a smile and laugh from their eleven-month old when Elin had been the one nursing and playing with him all day.

Mark scrolled through his phone, reading out funny tweets and showing her memes as she washed up Padarn's dinner things. Mark was so handsome, she thought, when he was happy. She hadn't seen him like this for years, not since they'd met at university, when they both worked at the student union bar. In those days, it was all about nights out in fancy dress, pre-drinks in halls, who fancied who, film nights in the communal space – where Mark would lounge attractively on the bean bags while keeping up a running commentary on whatever they happened to be watching. Elin had fallen in love with his dark brown hair, high cheekbones, elegant mouth. He was skinny then, but now he'd filled out with the meals she'd been cooking for him since they'd moved in together five years ago. He'd studied computer technology. Since then, he'd bounced around from one contract to another, before finally getting a full-time job in the field he did his dissertation on. The topic had been explained to her on several occasions, but she could never remember exactly. Something about video games, the ones you play online, killing monsters and demons... A dream job, in any case,

6

which is why they'd had to move from the west coast to the outskirts of Cardiff.

What did she study? It seemed like another lifetime; it had, in fact, been another lifetime. Another girl had gone to university, sat her exams, done well. Another girl had sat in the library, eager to get it right, put the best words on the page, the high marks. The grades – God. They had meant so much to her then. And now they were meaningless in the face of this overwhelming task. Padarn. Keeping Padarn alive and well.

Paddy burped into her ear as she picked him up and passed him over to Mark so she could go to the bathroom. Oh, how she loved the bathroom. It was so new, it gleamed; she hadn't needed to clean it yet.

"I'll put the cot together now if you like," Mark said when she returned. "Give you a chance to have a good night's sleep."

"Oh, okay." She'd got used to Paddy being back in their room, with the convenience of only needing to lean over to pop a dummy in his mouth. He cried less, knowing she was close. "If you've got the energy."

Sleep had been an enduring battle between Elin and Padarn, Mark and Padarn, Elin and Mark. In the old, one-bedroom flat above the bike shop, Mark insisted on putting the big cot in the kitchen-living-dining room. She refused, and they compromised by having the cot at the farthest end of their room. Every night, Paddy would cry at bedtime and, invariably, Mark would insist on leaving him to cry while Elin wanted to comfort him.

"He's got to learn," Mark said, over and over again.

Elin didn't disagree; it was simply too difficult for her to listen to her son's desperate weeping. Tonight, Mark's enthusiasm about putting the big, wooden cot together was an extension of this old battle. He wanted to get things going – the separate room for Padarn, the cry-to-sleep solution he stubbornly fought for. Fine, she thought.

Let him build it, but I'm not packing away the travel cot yet.

When, an hour later, she ascended the steps with the sleepy Padarn protesting in her arms, ready for his nightly cry, she saw that Mark had already dismantled the travel cot and put it in the attic.

*

That night Elin fell asleep on her own. Her husband was downstairs in the cramped dining room, working late, while her son was in a deep miraculous sleep down the hall. The double bed felt large, cold. The sheets were still musty from the move. She put her head beneath the covers and breathed in her own warm breath, curled up into herself, hands tucked into her sides, a parted, lonely being, far away from her mother and her sister and her college friends. Elin closed her eyes, rotating into blackness. She span, dizzy and melting, into sleep.

Or not quite sleep… Instead, she found herself sitting at her usual spot in the university library, working frantically. There was a deadline. A panic. She only had minutes left to finish her work. Between the stacks, she heard the whisperings of night workers, a rough sleeper, beings she could not see. The work had to be completed immediately. Before her on the table was a stretch of material like that of a scratch card. Furiously, she rubbed at it, so that it would reveal the words beneath, the quotations she needed for her essay, the solution to the assignment that she couldn't quite remember. The silvery material flaked off under her nails, and when she'd scratched and torn at it enough, she paused to look at what she'd uncovered. A red substance covered her hands: liquid garnet, dripping down her wrists. She realised that the surface she had been so furiously rubbing away was skin and, beneath it, raw flesh. The raw flesh belonged to her; was in fact, the tender expanse of her stomach, flayed open, and from somewhere above her head she heard someone screaming.

She woke to her son's cries: outraged, frantic. The kind of cries that accompanied his injections, or a bump to the head. Mark was asleep beside her, not stirring.

She got up, moving awkwardly in the dark, unaccustomed to the house, its edges and contours, catching her elbow on the door frame. The dream followed her along the dark hallway, the sharp horror of it, the shock. The nursery was the darkest room in the house on account of the blackout blinds she'd bought for the window, designed to encourage Padarn to sleep longer in the mornings. She fumbled around for the dummy first, but quickly gave up as his sobs grew more desperate. Then she took a while searching for the light-switch. By the time she found it, Padarn had become so upset he'd vomited on the sheets. Globules of milk and bile-coloured vegetable puree spattered in a halo round his head. His face was wet with tears; eyes screwed up tight, so she could only see the large red circle of his mouth, hollering. She picked him up, held him close to her chest, rocking him from side to side. None of it seemed to comfort him. She began to sing the lullaby he loved, and which her mother had often sung to her in the cradle.

> *Huna blentyn ar fy mynwes*
> *Clyd a chynnes ydyw hon*
> *Breichiau mam sy'n dynn amdanat*
> *Cariad mam dan fy mron*

> *Sleep my darling on my bosom*
> *Harm will never come to you*
> *Mother's arms enfold you safely*
> *A mother's love within my breast*

She sang it softly, close to his ear, twice-over so that its undulating, see-sawing rhythm could soothe him. Still, he cried. With one hand, she deftly stripped the cot and threw the dirty sheet in the laundry bag before carrying the disconsolate baby to their room. There, finally, he quietened. She placed Padarn on her side of the bed, gently, and away from her husband. Despite her best efforts, Mark woke up.

"What are you doing?" he hissed.

"He's ill," she said. "He was sick in the cot."

"You can't bring him in here. We'll never get him sleeping on his own if you do that."

"It's just for tonight, so I can keep an eye on him."

Padarn was already, impossibly, asleep. His breath on her face, smelling of curdled milk, his tiny hand curled around her thumb. Mark sighed and turned away.

*

The next day, while her husband was at work, Elin phoned the NHS helpline. They asked her: Does he have a temperature? No. How many times did he vomit? Just the once, she admitted. She was told to call back if anything changed. Although she'd hardly slept, Paddy didn't seem to be ill that morning. He was as irritable as he'd been since the move, but ate well, and latched onto her breast in the early hours of the day. A baby could throw up for any number of benign reasons, the NHS website informed her, and so there was no need to worry unduly. Keep an eye on him was the advice. So she did, as she did every day.

The unpacking was sadly over. Their belongings were few, and the house seemed quite empty with their things, whereas the old flat above the bike shop had been stuffed full. Now that everything was in its place, the white walls and grey carpets seemed somewhat cold to her.

"We'll have to put some pictures up," she told Paddy, who was lying on his stomach on the playmat. "Of you and Daddy and Mummy. What do you think? We'll have a big family one made when you're one. In a proper studio."

Elin spent the morning trying to motivate his walking with little success. She held him up under the armpits, encouraging him to move his feet, but he didn't last more than thirty seconds before his pudgy legs collapsed.

"Had enough is it?" she said. "Had enough already?"

'Conventional wisdom' – which ruled her daily life as a mother of a young child – said it was pointless to compare babies with each other. Every child develops at his or her own pace. Elin knew this to be true, yet she couldn't help comparing Padarn with her niece, who'd walked by ten months, or her friend's baby, who followed her mother everywhere by shuffling on her bum. Mark said Paddy relied too much on her; that she swooped in too fast in his playtime, not allowing him a chance to learn by himself. Yes, maybe that was right. But if she wasn't here he would cry, and she couldn't bear her son's sadness, even if they were only small sadnesses.

The nightmare came back to her then. That dream of flayed flesh, the vomit. Awful, she thought. And how tired she was now, struggling to keep up any enthusiasm while playing with Padarn. The dream shocked her deeply, even more, perhaps, than the speckles of vomit on Paddy's sheet. At least the latter was manageable and concrete. It reminded her of those first weeks after her son's birth: the extreme sleep deprivation, the waking nightmares. A doctor called them 'hallucinations', although she wouldn't go that far. In truth, she couldn't remember much of that time – couldn't say what had been real or dream – but the feeling haunted her still. The feeling of being trapped; not being able to see the end to the pain. All the different

11

pains of that time. She could still list them: the pain of insomnia, the pain in her breasts, the pains across her belly, the pains of inadequacy and terror that accompanied the presence of the tiny, wailing newborn. She'd been plagued by images of drowning, being torn apart by sea creatures, being buried alive. The dreams had been bad then. But they'd retreated thanks to the prescribed medication and the week she spent in the Mother and Baby Unit. She hadn't thought it possible the visions could return.

It was just the move, she thought. New surroundings. They say moving to a new house is one of the most stressful events of adult life, don't they? Don't be so hard on yourself.

She decided to make herself a coffee and take Paddy outside into the clear, bright day. Enjoy her little son and her new home.

"Shall we go outside? Say hello to Mr Sun?"

The garden was the only part of the house the property developer hadn't touched. A narrow plot of wilderness with two dark imposing fir trees at the far end. Weeds and voluminous, prickly-looking bushes dominated, with a few patches of dried earth at the front where, perhaps, the developer had attempted to clear up. The fence had been repainted a gleaming white; it was not particularly high, and she could easily peer at the neighbour's serene, well-tended lawn. Across the fence: borders of purple and pink flowers framed the lawn, and a perfectly even patio jutted out into the cut grass. It made her think of the lovely things they might do with their own garden. She had seen her neighbours once or twice through the kitchen window – two women, sitting out in the afternoons, drinking what she assumed was lemonade from tall glasses. One was very elderly and the other around Elin's mother's age.

Just as she was thinking about them, one of the neighbours appeared. She'd clearly been working in the garden. There was mud on her knees and a sheen of sweat on her face. Elin smiled, went to introduce herself with Paddy on her hip, pulling at her hair.

"What a darling!" The neighbour said.

The neighbour approached the fence, a small shovel in one hand and something else in the other. Her long greying hair was clipped back to make way for a green visor. Sixty? Sixty-five? She seemed solid and strong, with the shovel in her hand and that thing in the other.

"How old is he?"

"Just gone eleven months."

"What a darling," she said again.

Paddy managed to tear some of his mother's hair out. "Ouch!"

"They can be little monsters, though, can't they?"

"Yeah," she said, batting Paddy's hands away. "I'm Elin."

"Georgina." The neighbour smiled. "You'll have to tell him off. Teach him it's wrong."

"Bit young for that," Elin said, her eyes landing on the drooping, muddy thing the old woman was holding.

"Not my business, of course. You on your own?"

"No," Elin said, staring at the dangling brown sack. "My husband's working."

"He's still going out to work, is he? With this virus going round?"

But Elin was distracted. "Sorry," she said, "is that what I think it is?"

"What, this?" Georgina lifted the thing up. "It's a rat. A dead one."

Elin stepped back. "Oh."

"The bugger was hiding in my compost bin. I've tried to catch him a couple of times before, but today I succeeded as you can see." She shook the shovel in victory, and Elin's stomach turned. The reason she hadn't recognised the rat was because it was missing its head. The red-white stump

13

gleamed in the sun.

Georgina sighed. "Strange times, isn't it?"

"Yes, very strange."

"Still, I'm so pleased you've moved in. It's lovely to have neighbours again."

Elin realised then that she didn't know how long the house had been empty before the developer had bought it, or anything about who had lived here before. The neighbour seemed to read her mind. "No one's lived there for years," she said. "The nice gentleman came in and got rid of all the old rubbish. Put it all in a skip. Avocado bathroom and carpets thick with dust. Hadn't been anyone looking after it."

"Do you remember who lived there before, then?"

"A family, it was. They were nice. Well, she was. About your age. They had children too."

"Did they move away then?"

Georgina glanced up at the house. Her expression seemed tense suddenly; a deep crease appeared between her eyes and a dark flush spread across her cheeks. "Yes, I think so."

"Where to?"

The neighbour moved to go back inside, swinging the dead rat breezily back and forth. "I don't know. England somewhere."

"Oh."

"Look. Elin, is it? I'd better be off. Mam will be asking for her tea. She's ninety-eight but still has all her teeth. If you see her, don't get scared. Her eyes are that way because she refuses to go under the knife. She hates needles and doesn't trust doctors. Had all her children in the front room." The woman gave the rat one last swing, turning to the side. There was a spatter of blood on the back of her trousers the size of a handprint. "Pleasure to meet you."

"Yes," Elin said. "Pleasure."

14

*

Later that day, in the midst of the usual evening chores, Elin thought little about the neighbour. Neither did she pay much heed to the news of the virus, because she didn't listen to the news or, if she did, it was always in the background, reaching her from afar with an occasional phrase or word. Her mind was jumpy these days – it had been like that since the birth. She couldn't fix on one idea or the other. Any thought she had would be interrupted by an equally urgent thought about what she had to do next, or later, or tomorrow. There were lists strewn across the new house: shopping lists, to do-lists, reminders. She crossed off the tasks slowly and added new ones quickly. The early evening was her busiest time of day, with Mark arriving home at six, starving hungry, and the little one about to have his bath and bedtime. She rushed upstairs and downstairs a hundred times, fetching things, forgetting things.

They didn't eat together. Mark warmed up his plate in the microwave while she took care of the bath. She would eat a snack later if she wasn't too tired. In the first week, in high spirits from his job, Mark wolfed down his food and came up to help. Paddy giggled in delight when his father lifted him out of the bath and held his dimply naked body against his chest, laying him down again on the makeshift nappy station Elin set up on their bed. Mark tickled him there, sang half-remembered nursery rhymes and some he made up on the spot while Elin dressed the baby.

"Don't excite him too much now," she said, smiling.

"He loves it," Mark said. "Don't you? You smelly sausage. You enormous poo factory. You silly poo dinosaur."

Yes, that had been in the first week of March. But that

evening, only nine days since their move, Mark returned home sullen and withdrawn.

"Everything alright, cariad?" she asked, coming downstairs after managing to settle Padarn in his cot. "Did something happen at work?"

"No. Why do you think that?"

"I don't. I'm asking what's wrong, that's all."

"Nothing's wrong."

"Okay." She took his dirty plate to the sink. "We don't have to talk if you don't want to."

He sat hunched over the kitchen table, staring at a spot on the floor. Elin pretended not to notice; he would talk when he was ready, she thought. The worst thing for either of them was an argument. After sleepless nights, and the dead rat, an argument was the last thing she wanted, so she kept to the sink, washing every utensil within arm's reach. After eating, Mark shut himself in the dining room – the small room that held no furniture. A moment later he went to fetch his laptop, charger, and a couple of sofa cushions, and closed the door.

She dried her hands on the tea towel. Right, she thought. It would be impossible for her to relax, knowing that he was in there, upset and unwilling to speak. There had been times in the past – before she knew him – when he'd done stupid things. Elin's mother-in-law had drawn her to one side on two occasions to explain that Mark needed someone caring, attentive; that he'd been liable to mood swings as a child; that he'd been thrown out of several schools as a result of misunderstandings. He had a therapist, she'd explained, to work through his anger. What anger? Elin remembered saying. That was then, at college, when Mark had been joyful and carefree. "Children react to events in ways you wouldn't expect," his mother said. "They feel the world in a different way. Thin-skinned, you know. I think Mark's still like that really, deep inside. A sensitive soul. You'll be careful, won't you?"

Elin never discovered what had made Mark angry as
a child or sensitive as an adult; in fact, at the time, she'd
thought his mother was simply marking her territory in the
way mothers do with their grown-up sons: letting her know
that Elin could never be as close to Mark as she was. But
now, after five years together and two years of marriage,
she knew her mother-in-law had been sincere.

She knocked on the door. "Mark? Babes?"

"What is it?"

"Just checking you're okay." She eased the door open a
fraction. "Can I come in?"

"Sure."

He was sitting on the floor, back against the wall,
computer on his lap. The lights were off, the laptop screen
illuminated his face in an electric glow.

"Babes, what's going on?"

He shrugged. "It's just...stuff."

"What stuff?"

"This virus crap."

"Oh, yeah," she said. "Well, it'll be okay, won't it? We're
young and Paddy spends most of his time at home with me
anyway."

"I'm not worried about you and the baby."

"Oh."

"I didn't mean it like that. I meant... Forget about it."

"No. Go on, please."

"What if they have to close the office?"

"Are they talking about closing the office?"

"Potentially."

"You can work here, right? You said yourself that most
of what you do can be done from home. You'd miss your
new work mates, I guess, but otherwise..."

"It's not the same," he snapped. "You don't get it."

"We could make this into a nice office. A chair and a

17

desk. We'll make sure not to disturb you. I can bring you your lunch, if you want."

"Chair and desk? With what money?"

"I'll buy it for you. It'll be my gift."

"Elin, you don't have a job. Don't be ridiculous."

"It's going to be okay. It'll be temporary."

"Yeah." Mark leaned his head back against the wall, not meeting her eyes. "Yeah."

"Do you want a cuddle?"

He looked askance at her. For a moment, she was afraid he would refuse. But then he closed the laptop and raised his arms, like Paddy did when he wanted to be picked up, and she went to him, clasping him close, his lips against her neck, the hard pressure of his arms on her back, pulling her down into his embrace.

"I love you," she murmured into his hair.

"I love you too."

*

The peace didn't last. The virus dominated the news; even Elin could no longer ignore it. Her family called her, told her to take care of herself and Paddy, and urged her to stay indoors.

"Where do you think I go?" She asked her mam. "I don't know anyone here."

"Tell Mark to wear a mask at work," her mam insisted.

She laughed. "Yeah, right!"

"I'm serious."

"What about you? Are you staying home like you should?"

"Of course I am. Your sister's bringing me food and leaving it on the doorstep. Your Da and me aren't setting foot outside until this horribleness goes away."

Elin thought, well, I do that anyway. Stay in. See no one.

The only difference the lockdown makes is that now I don't have the smallest chance for a life outside the house. All the baby groups stopped meeting. The local leisure centre was shut. Lockdown is life with a small baby, she wanted to text her sister, but her sister was so competent, so sociable and energetic, that having two children had never stopped her from doing everything she wanted. It was only Elin, it seemed, who found child-rearing difficult and isolating. Only Elin who felt nothing but trepidation when going to the supermarket with Paddy at her side.

Still, it wasn't her mother or her sister or even her son she was worried about. Mark's mood had worsened since that night. The dining room floor became his habitual retreat – a place where he could shield her from his worst spells, and where she learned not to disturb him. The office would close on Monday the 23rd of March. He had two days to sort out his affairs, save the necessary files, empty his drawers. He'd only just arrived, and already he brought back the framed photograph of the three of them he had on his desk.

"This is shit," he said, when he produced the photograph from his bag. "Completely shit."

"I know, cariad. I know."

"Thing is, I don't know if you do know."

She swerved this comment, preferring to steam Paddy's vegetables for the following day. It would be like this for a week or so, she thought. Fine. She was prepared to carry the brunt of his disappointment. The job had meant so much to him. The prospect of it alone had lifted him out of misery six months earlier, when he'd been turned down after his ninth interview. It was proof that he was not, in his words, 'fucking worthless'. He'd sworn a lot back then – in front of Paddy, too, which he never did when he was his normal, contented self. The swearing wore her down unexpectedly, because it wasn't used for comic effect, or for emphasis, or any ordinary speech. The fucks and cunts and shitheads were reserved for his anger and hatred of certain people. She'd almost forgotten how he'd speak like that when he was sad, but now it was back. "Completely fucking shit. I mean, are you even listening?" he asked her.

"Course I am."

"You don't get it."

"I do get it. It's really bad, I know. But there's nothing we can do about it right now."

"You know that we can't actually afford this house without the job, right?"

"I know," she said. "Babes, they're not firing you. You just have to work from home for a while."

"You don't understand. Everything's closing down. Everything. The business isn't going to get any fucking customers. They haven't got any fucking money coming in. If they don't have any money coming in, how the fuck are they going to pay me?"

Elin sliced the cauliflower head in two with a large knife, before snapping off its white branches. "Have they said they're not going to pay you?"

"Not in so many words."

"Then it's going to be fine."

"It's not."

"Okay."

"Okay what?"

"Just okay!" She wiped the knife on her apron. "I'm sorry. It's a bad situation."

"Am I annoying you?"

"No."

"Do you want to get rid of me?"

"Yes, I want to throw you and Paddy out on the street. Then I'm going to steal the car, drive to Majorca and live in a beach hut." She saw his frown. "God, Mark! I'm only kidding."

"Ha-ha," he said, picking up his phone. "Funny."

*

In the early hours, she woke to her son shrieking. She shot out of bed, her entire body taut, wide awake, as though she'd been waiting for this all night. She moved so quickly in the darkness that she stubbed her toe badly on the landing. In the nursery, she groped for the cot in the dark, trying to find the dummy. Padarn wailed as she searched, but no luck. "Shhh, shhh," she said. "Wait now. Wait a moment." A sensation crept over her; she had the strange feeling that something, or someone was causing her son's distress: a presence in the darkness.

Elin hit the light switch.

Paddy had pushed himself onto his side, his face close to the bars of the cot, eyes rolling upwards. For a moment, she just stood there, taking it in. She'd never seen him contort himself in the cot like this before. Was it some kind of fit? His hands on the bars suggested this was not the case. And his expression... It was too knowing for a sick baby, too aware. He was trying to look at the far corner, which was why his eyes were rolling. The far corner of his empty room. His mouth was agape, his skin flushed with sobbing, saliva and tears streaking his face.

"Dere di. Dere di!" Poor little thing. Poor thing, like her grandmother used to say. She tried to scoop him up, but his hands gripped the bars tight. Again, his expression... She wasn't sure what it was. There was something about it that was unfamiliar, disconcerting. What was he looking at? They didn't have any furniture for the nursery, except the cot. They stored all his toys downstairs in IKEA boxes. The walls were perfectly white. No shadows could appear there, either, as the room was always dark – so dark that you couldn't see your own hand, just as the baby books advised.

Elin peeled his fingers away from the bars and held him close. Walking towards the far corner, he began to wail louder and bury his face in her chest. She stood there and viewed the quiet, inoffensive room: his nice little cot with the blue striped sleeping bag, the handmade mobile of stuffed animals her sister had gifted him. Paddy began pummelling her chest with his hands.

"But there's nothing here, little one. There's nothing here."

He wouldn't be comforted. So she brought him into their bed where, nestled between her breast and her arm, he fell asleep. As usual, she tried to do it as quietly as possible. And yet she heard Mark mutter, "Not again."

Elin hardly slept. She kept on seeing her baby in front of her, in that strange posture, like a prisoner pushing his face against the railings, and his expression was like a prisoner too. Like someone on death row, watching the jailer coming for them. She realised then what it was – that new thing she'd witnessed in her baby. Fear.

*

The day was bright and cool. Elin was grateful for the sunlight, the way it streamed into the kitchen, opening the space by reflecting the white walls. A welcome antidote to the night.

Paddy spent the day on the verge of tears. She blamed the bad nights of sleep and the crying fits and sudden night-time separation that Mark had enforced. Elin didn't care to think too much about the strange position she'd found him in, or the fear on his infant face. Paddy continued to cling to her, complained when she lay him down on the playmat or encouraged him to crawl by waving toys in front of him. In the end, she dug out the old sling they'd used when he was a newborn, strapped him to her chest, his legs dangling against her abdomen, his fat

22

cheek on her collarbone. He calmed and slept.

Although he was heavy, and her back ached, at least she could get some of the housework done. Elin planned to make a nice meal that night, knowing that Mark would come home depressed from his last day of office work. She worried he'd be set on an argument unless she did something to distract him. Not only would an elaborate meal cheer him up, it would also serve as a kind of shield: look, this is what I do for you. This is how I love you. So she went to the local supermarket, where suspicious, glove-wearing shoppers furtively piled their trolleys with pasta and tins. She bought the ingredients she needed for a lasagne – half pork, half beef, with a homemade béchamel and garlic bread – and spent the afternoon chopping and stirring at the stove, with Paddy alternatively asleep and wriggling in the sling.

She was missing dried herbs: basil, oregano. They'd entirely slipped her mind in the quiet panic of the supermarket aisles. The garden was a wilderness, yet she remembered seeing, directly in front of the heavy firs that grew at the far end, a bay tree.

It was good to be outside, in any case. The breeze cooled her skin, flushed from the cooking steam. She'd been putting off going outside in case she met Georgina again – the memory of the headless rat revolted her more now than it had when she'd first encountered it. Thankfully, the neighbour was nowhere to be seen.

Bits of rubbish were strewn at the back of the garden: crisp packets that had been blown in, an old, decaying tennis ball. She collected it and put it to one side. It was difficult to bend down with Padarn, but she managed to tie the sling so that he was hugging her hip rather than her chest. There were dandelions, thistles, daisies, a few buttercups; the glint of spiderwebs in the sunlight, weaving between the lower branches of the trees. Why had the previous owner decided to plant firs? Elin thought. Tall,

ragged, green towers that sucked up all light: a wall of
plant-mass. As she went near, she heard the low buzzing of
flies and saw the round gristly bellies of the spiders. There
was a smell, too, neither green nor fresh, but a smell like a
dank prison cell. At the base of one of the trees, just out
of the way of its light-blocking branches, was the bay tree.
She took a handful of leaves, before going closer to the firs,
exploring what might be growing there at the very back of
the garden. There were a few more straggly plants that had
been left to wither under the shadow of the trees. Grass
turned into a thick carpet of dead needles, rust brown,
studded with more fragments of foil and plastic. She
started picking up the rubbish and putting it in her back
pocket. A bottle top. Plastic wrap. A broken key chain. A
glimpse of white skin.

Elin shot up in time to see something pale vanishing
between the trees: a flicker of limbs. A ripple ran along the
branches as though a body had brushed past.

A neighbour, Elin thought quickly. It must have been one
of the women from next door. The firs were so thick, she
wasn't sure what was behind them; or whether there was
any wall or fence separating the two gardens. But then why
didn't they say anything? A sensation came over her again
from the night before: the feeling that she was not alone;
that she was being watched by someone in the trees. Elin
gripped the bay leaves tight in her hands; she didn't move.
Didn't breathe.

It's nothing, she thought quickly. I saw nothing. The fir
trees seemed to gather together, menacing and violent, like
a phalanx of soldiers. It was the light. It's because I am so,
so tired.

She was about to leave when she spotted a glimmer of
metal among the dead pine needles. A small silver head,
sticking out of the earth. Elin pulled at it, retrieving an
alien-looking orange action figure, with bendable arms and

24

legs, seventies in its style and colouring. She considered adding it to the pile of garden rubbish she'd accrued but, in the end, thought better of it. She'd show it to Mark. A vintage toy like that could be worth something.

She walked swiftly back to the house, through the long grass, trying desperately to leave the memory of the pale thing in the trees behind her. On her way back to the kitchen, she risked a peek into the neighbours' garden. There, on the patio, sat an elderly lady who, she realised, must be Georgina's mother. The woman had her slippered feet up on an upturned flowerpot, two Welsh carthens thrown over her lap and shoulders so that her body was swathed in cloth, invisible. Her eyes were closed, napping into the afternoon, and by the wizened face and wispy, balding head, she seemed to Elin to be hundreds of years old.

*

Mark didn't come home until past midnight. The lasagne was in the oven for hours, solidifying into a mass of fat. Paddy went to sleep at eight. Without Mark there to supervise the bedtime, she'd allowed Padarn to fall asleep in her arms, before gently laying him down in his cot. She thought of going to bed herself but felt she should be there when he returned. Phone calls went unanswered, although she could see by his WhatsApp that he'd been online recently, so she hadn't been worried for his safety, exactly. She sat on the sofa, alone, not knowing what to do with herself. Eventually, there was the sound of the key in the lock, and Mark stumbled in, smelling of beer.

"You've been to the pub?"

He didn't say anything, scrabbled around with his keys and rucksack, shrugged off his jacket.

"Mark," she said.

"Yeah?"

"It's late."

"So?"

"Why didn't you call?"

"Do I have to call? Isn't it obvious that I'd go out for a few drinks with my colleagues while we still can? They're going to close the pubs next week."

"You can do what you like, but just let me know."

He winced as though she'd hurt him. "Do you have to stand there like that? Accosting me in the hallway?" He said, pushing past her to the kitchen.

"I made a lasagne," she said. "Are you hungry?"

"I ate at the pub."

"Did you?"

"Yeah. Nuts and crap."

"I'll warm up a bit for you."

"Don't want it."

She leaned against the door frame, watching him take a can out of the fridge. Her limbs felt heavy, her eyelids... When was the last time she'd slept properly, deeply? Months. Years. He drank with his back to her. How had it come to this? Like a scene from a fifties' novel, a marriage-on-the-rocks scene, the downbeat housewife, her laboured-over meal cold and ignored, and the husband back too late from the pub. God, she didn't care about the pub. She didn't care about the lasagne. She didn't want to be this kind of woman – defined by the meals she cooked and the house she kept, dependent on the moods and whims of her husband. She straightened up. "Whatever," she said. "I'm going to bed."

"Wait. I know you brought him into our bed again last night. Don't do it, okay? Just don't. It's stupid. It's counter-productive."

"He was scared."

"Babies aren't afraid of the dark. He doesn't know

enough about the world to be afraid of anything."

"He had a nightmare."

"Babies don't have nightmares. Their sleep is, like, dreamless."

"How do you know?"

"It's a scientific fact," he said, annoyed. "Babies don't dream."

They don't dream, but they can see, she thought. They react. "Babies are afraid," she ventured. "He's afraid when he thinks we're going to drop him. He throws his arms out and his whole body goes stiff."

"That's just a reflex, for God's sake. I thought you knew about this stuff? Jesus," he said. "Don't bring him into the bed. We'll be sleeping with a fucking six-year-old if you keep doing that."

"Fine," she said, but he'd already turned away from her, disappearing into the dining room behind the closed door where, she assumed, he would sit on the floor to drink his beer in the light of his laptop.

*

Whether Padarn dreamt or not, she couldn't say, but she did. In her dream, she shared her bed with the old woman from next door, like she had done with her grandmother when she was a very young girl. Elin could only make out the closed eyes of the old woman and tufts of long white hair. Panic took over her, because they were trapped, almost paralysed, in the bed, and there was another person in the room with them. Someone she couldn't see yet, but she knew was coming. She knew like a child knows when his mother is distressed. A bad thing was about to happen, and there was nothing she could do about it. The flannel covers were so tight she could not move her head to one side. The thing came closer, closer, and the old woman didn't stir.

A thought took her: perhaps the old woman's already dead beneath the covers? And the heat is not her body's warmth, but the warmth of her blood, leaving her body?

Wake up, she told herself. Wake up now. I do not want to see this.

No.

He was coming. He was here, in the room. He would do them both harm. He was coming for her, just as he had come for his own children.

Wake up. Wake up.

The flash of metal. The crunch of broken bone. A caved-out face. Pieces of tongue and cartilage in her mouth.

Elin's eyes fluttered. There. Her room, thank God. Her room and her snoring husband who had managed to find his way to bed. She lay there for a while, grateful that the nightmare was over.

And then a new kind of panic... It was strange, she thought, to be awake without hearing Padarn crying. It was four-thirty. The house was silent. She listened carefully, in a way a parent listens in a house, attuned to each breath and moan. Silence. Then why was she awake – was it the nightmare? No. It wasn't that. There was something wrong in the house. She could sense it in the quietness. The baby monitor showed the outline of a white shape – his blanket – nothing more.

She went to the nursery, her phone light in one hand. She put her ear to the door and listened carefully for his breath.

There. She could hear it, coming and going, coming and going. Good, she thought.

And then a gurgling. Drawn out, like a light, childlike growl at the back of the throat. Her heart went cold. She was sure that this gurgling could not be her baby.

There, his breaths. There, the drawn-out gurgling that sounded almost like an adult, or an animal. Something was not right; the gurgling and the breathing were not in-sync. It was as though there were two babies, making sounds at the same time.

Despite the promise to her husband, she opened the door, torchlight directed towards the ground so as not to wake Padarn.

Her baby was on the floor. He was crawling away from her, towards the far corner. How was it possible? Padarn couldn't crawl; she had never seen him even attempt it. Not only that, but he was moving fast, as though trying to get away. There was something guilty in his movements, furtive. She dropped her phone in shock and the light swept upwards to the ceiling, revealing Padarn in the cot, asleep, in that eerily silent, deep sleep that babies reach. He hadn't, then, been crawling on the floor, towards the far corner, because he was here and could not crawl; could not, of course, get out of the cot.

Elin's heart was racing. Perhaps I'm still dreaming, she thought. Sometimes dreams do that; they cross over into the real world.

Padarn was sleeping peacefully, despite the sharp light from her phone. She didn't want to leave him there alone. So she fetched a pillow and a blanket from the spare room and lay down on the floor where her husband found her the next morning.

*

The next day Mark's fears were realised. He was furloughed – a word Elin had never heard before, and now heard everywhere – his pay reduced. The dining room did indeed become a study, as Elin predicted, but Mark refused her offer of desk and chair, preferring to save money.

Instead, he told her that he would work extra hours, trying to find freelance work so they could keep up with the mortgage.

"Good idea," she said. "If you want, I can find some part time work?"

"Who would look after Padarn?"

"You," she said.

"But what you earn in a supermarket isn't going to be the same as what I could earn freelancing," he said. "It just doesn't make economic sense."

"Okay."

She didn't tell him about the crawling figure she'd seen the night before, or the gurgling noises that had emanated from the nursery. It had been a dream, or a dream extension. Not, she told herself, a hallucination. Although later, while Padarn napped, she looked up the symptoms of post-natal depression again. She asked Google: can it resurface? Can you get it again, months later? Not that she'd had it that bad to begin with. The days she'd spent in the Mother and Baby Unit had been overkill. Her husband... God! She'd been furious with him for throwing her so easily at the mercy of psychiatrists and doctors. She hated the medication they gave her, and the patronising way they asked how she was feeling. The only good thing about the hospital was the sleep. She had slept. Days and days she'd slept, so that she had no sense, anymore, how much time she'd actually spent there. The online picture was not particularly reassuring: postnatal depression can affect women in different ways. It can start at any point in the first year after giving birth and may develop suddenly or gradually. Out of the list of symptoms, however, she was pleased that she had neither low mood nor loss of interest, suicidal thoughts or problems making decisions. Apart from guilt – and who didn't feel guilty? – she had none of the other symptoms. Good, she thought, before remembering the apparition of the night before. The crawling baby. What was that, if not my mind going?

It's just the move, she told herself. All this upheaval. The pandemic. There are things in the press – Covid dreams, they're calling it. Everyone's getting them. Anxiety manifested.

Padarn's morning nap grew from the usual thirty minutes to over two hours. It was as though he hadn't slept at all the night before, the way he was sprawled across the sofa, arms thrown back.

"You have a good sleep now," she whispered to him.

And so he slept. He slept while she made the oat and banana pancakes he liked; he slept while she watched television; he slept when she put him down on the playmat, and when she sang to him, and when she held him aloft in the air. He was awake enough to drink his milk, eat a little of the pancakes, before resting his head back against the highchair and falling asleep.

She called the helpline again. No temperature. No fever. No vomit. No crying. No rashes.

"He seems to be sleeping a lot," she said.

"Right, okay. He's not floppy?"

She paused. "No." In fact, he was solid against her, as tense as her own body.

"See how he is. Keep an eye on him," they told her.

In the garden, waiting out the long afternoon with her sleeping boy, while her husband was shut away in his 'study', she thought again about that other baby. The crawling one. She remembered how fast it had moved, as though it had done something bad. It was as if it had stolen something from her baby, then fled the scene. The gurgles that were so unlike her own baby's sweet noises had been lower, older-sounding, threatening even. No wonder Padarn had been so afraid. Padarn was still asleep. The deep near-silent sleep that had, at one time, when he was only a few weeks old, scared her into staying awake and watching over him. Now months later she found herself doing it again.

*

In the evening, close to bedtime, he finally woke up, but was very unhappy about it. He sobbed in her arms, cried when she changed his nappy. He pushed his little fat arms against her chest, twisted his head back in startling sobs.

"What's got into him?" asked Mark, who'd emerged from his makeshift study to warm up supper in the microwave. "Is he ill?"

"Don't think so. I phoned the helpline, but they said just to keep an eye on him."

That's what they always say, she wanted to add, but she didn't want to complain about anything in case he got annoyed with her.

Perhaps Padarn was really ill? The vomiting of a few days before an early symptom? But he seemed strong and healthy, physically speaking. In the rare times her baby had been ill in the past, he'd also become clingy, like this, it was true; yet he'd also been feverish, prone to drifting in and out of sleep, his voice weak and wheezing. Mark gave an exasperated sigh: it meant that she should get the baby upstairs, quietly.

But when she reached the nursery, Padarn became even more inconsolable, grabbing at her hair, pulling the collar of her shirt. "Okay, okay. Calm down."

She put her hand on his chest, did the rhythmic long shushes that would, eventually, lull him to sleep. He calmed slightly, although his hands gripped hers as if willing her to stay. He looked, again, at the far corner of the room, where there was nothing but the white walls, the edge of the blacked-out window. He craned his head back in order to see, swivelling his large grey-blue eyes that were like her own. It was as though he were looking for someone, she thought. The shadow-baby she'd seen the night before, stealing away from his cot.

"Dere di. Dere di," she said in the language her mamgu had spoken to her when she was his age, before singing the lullaby. "Huna blentyn ar fy mynwes... Ni wna undyn â thi gam." Sleep child on my bosom, no harm will ever come to you...

Elin stayed until his eyes closed and his hands fell away from her own. It took a long time, her back stiff and aching when she finally straightened up. She left the door ajar, so she could easily hear any sounds in the night. But when her husband came up, around midnight, he clicked the door shut.

*

Huna blentyn ar fy mynwes
Clyd a chynnes ydyw hon

Her mamgu had sung it to her mother in the cradle, and Mam to her. Lullabies and nursery rhymes, she'd learned, were ancient; passed down the generations, over hundreds of years. The singing reassured her as much as it did Padarn. It made her feel less alone, connected to her mam and mamgu and great-grandmothers through the act of lulling her child to sleep. It made her feel like a good mother as long as the song lasted, maternal and competent. Now she was in bed, the song wouldn't leave her mind. Again and again, the opening verse played, crushing all her other thoughts, like a dead weight on the front of her brain. Kicking the duvet off, she lay sprawled across the bed, waiting for Mark to come up and find her there, in an unusual position, forcing him to ask her how she was for a change.

But he didn't come up. He wouldn't come until midnight or the early hours. The failure to sleep, although all was quiet in the house, caused her heart to beat faster. She was scared; scared of slipping back into her old illness. I shouldn't have looked it up, she told herself. They tell you, don't they? Don't Google your symptoms. It scared her and yet, at the same time, she didn't really believe she was getting ill again. Those five weeks after Padarn's birth were indescribable, even as she tried repeatedly to describe it to herself on nights such as this. Suffocated, she thought, I felt suffocated. The birth had been difficult... It was typical, she was told, in cases like hers. The birth trauma – the psychiatrist liked this word 'trauma' – likely contributed to her feelings of powerlessness and claustrophobia. In the Mother and Baby Unit, Padarn was brought to her at certain hours and she was allowed to visit him at any time, although not at night. At night, her job was to sleep. Insomnia damages your brain. It makes it do strange things, she was told by nurses who didn't speak in the same technical terms as their doctored colleagues. Although Elin hated it there, the strict routine, the little paper cups filled with tablets, the bad food, it didn't compare to the birth and the five terrifying weeks that followed. They discharged her from the hospital the day after. Forceps delivery in the operating room. When he was born his soft head had been so deformed by the instruments he hardly looked human, more like a changeling, elongated, his face crushed and purple, his lip and ear mysteriously cut.

The midwives said "these things happen," but Padarn was slow to latch, slow to feed. In the days after, he fed and fed. She could not sleep, because he was attached to her breast. Her nipples bled into his mouth and when he sucked, a pain arose, like needles stabbing deep into her breasts. She did not sleep, because he cried and needed her; and when he slept, she had to eat, wash, cook. Mark was working at that time; her mother and sister, too, although they both offered to take time off. She refused.

No, she said, I will do it myself. You did it, she'd said to her sister. If you can do it, I can do it.

It wasn't possible, it turned out. She couldn't do it by herself. She cried every day, all day. She cried when she discovered a Baby-On-Board badge in her coat pocket; cried remembering how easy everything had been when her son had still been inside her, comfortable, quiet, feeding in a way that did not cause her agony.

"It's like torture," she said to the health visitor.

"Oh dear," she'd replied. "It's not supposed to hurt."

Elin never spoke about the pain again. The depression – the psychiatrist called it a depression, although it was not characterised by sadness, for her, but by an overwhelming sense of guilt and self-denigration. I should not be doing this. Why did they let me leave the hospital? Why did they think I could keep him alive? She had nightmares while her eyes were still open and she was feeding her child. Nightmares where dark shapes came and stole the baby away. Or where a great wave came and drowned them both while her family looked on. Or where her own baby began to suck her blood through her breasts until she died.

She did not remember the event that finally prompted Mark to seek help; neither did she remember being admitted to the Mother and Baby Unit. She had, occasionally, thought of asking him, only she'd never felt strong enough to hear the answer.

> *Huna blentyn ar fy mynwes*
> *Clyd a chynnes ydyw hon*

That song. It was still echoing in her head, still pulling its words through her mind. She sat up, suddenly. It wasn't in her mind. It was being sung. She was singing it; it was her voice. The notes drifted towards her from the nursery. Her voice from when she'd sang it a few hours ago, she was sure of it. Only she was not singing it now.

"No," she whispered. "Not this."

She went to the nursery, intent on saving her son from whatever was happening in that room, when she was stopped by a figure on the stairs.

"Mark."

"What are you doing?" He whispered. There was a bitterness to his breath. Whisky, she thought.

"Just checking on him."

"Why? He's not crying."

"Just quickly."

"You've got the monitor."

The monitor's useless, she wanted to say, but stopped herself. "I'll be quick."

"Elin, don't." He stepped between her and the door, blocking her way. In the background she could still hear the eerie echo of her own voice singing Huna blentyn. "Please, Mark. Just once, I promise. Please."

"He's not even fucking crying. Leave it."

The lullaby quickened pace, as though gearing up for a climax, louder and faster the words beat into her ears. She tried to push Mark out of the way, but he retaliated by grabbing her wrists, pushing her back into the bedroom.

"Stop it," he hissed. "Stop. Leave him alone."

"No," she said. "Get your hands off me. You don't understand. Get off!"

Mark kicked the bedroom door shut, put his face close to Padarn's. "He's fine, Elin. He's going to be fine, you just need to let him sleep."

"He's not well. He's not safe."

"Not safe? What do you mean?"

She paused. She couldn't tell Mark about the voice she was hearing – her own voice singing. She couldn't tell him about what she'd seen the night before either. He would think she was mad. He would take her to the Mother and Baby Unit again. The song was so fast now she could barely differentiate the words. The lyrics melting into each other to produce one, long insistent wail. Padarn was in there. Defenceless.

"Please," is all she could manage. Her arms went limp in his grip; she sank to her knees. "Please, Mark. Please let me go to him."

"This is for your own good, I promise," he said, as gently as he could, touching her cheek with his hand. "You'll realise he doesn't need you hovering over him every night. He'll sleep much better, and so will you. Sweetheart. Babes. I promise."

"No."

"Yes," he said, kissing the top of her head. "Do you trust me?"

She nodded: the lullaby had stopped. The quietness eerie in its completeness.

"Everything's okay," she told herself.

"Exactly. Everything is fine."

It was fine. Yes. In the morning, Padarn was still asleep and she had to wake him, but when his eyes opened, she was relieved to find him hungry. As she turned to leave with the baby in her arms, she spotted something on the ground. She paused to look closer. A small indentation in the plush, grey carpet on either side of the cot, as if it had been jolted to one side, leaving a mark where its legs had once been. Maybe I moved it when I put him down last night, or Mark might have checked on him in the morning... She paused again. A flash of orange. She bent down again and retrieved, from under the cot, the orange-and-silver action toy she'd found in the garden the other day. There were traces of soil, still, in the joints. She could only wonder at it for a moment, because Padarn was bellowing to be fed.

"In a minute, bach. In a minute now."

She took him to their bedroom, lay down on her side and lifted her shirt. She lay down so that she could think. The toy was still in her hand. How had it got into the room? Mark, she thought. But why? Or did I do it? Did I bring it upstairs by mistake? She thought she'd put it in the kitchen drawer, but perhaps she misremembered it, or she'd opened the drawer but forgotten to actually put the toy inside. These things sometimes happened; it was because she was so distracted, that was all. Once, she'd gone to the supermarket, filled the trolley in with a huge weekly shop, only to discover she'd left her purse and handbag at home. When she left the store promising to return with her credit card, she realised she'd locked her keys in the car...

Instead of slowing down, Paddy seemed to become increasingly hungry. He sucked harder and harder, until she winced and tried to push him away. This only upset him, causing him to claw at her breast, biting down on her nipple. "Ow! What the hell?" She stuck her finger in his mouth, breaking the latch. A pinprick of blood oozed out of her aureole. "Padarn bach, what did you do that for?" But despite the violence of her reaction, Padarn didn't cry. He looked at her balefully, almost as though he were as confused by his behaviour as she was. "Paddy bach," she said again, holding him close, but not allowing him to suckle. "You're safe with me. You're safe with your mam here. I love you. I love you."

If Mark came in now, she wouldn't be able to explain the tears running down her face. It was Padarn – how sweet and innocent he was! What had she done to him, pushing him away from her like that? What had happened that caused his desperation for her? The need to be close to her; to bite instead of suck, to bury his face in her breast. "Cariad bach. My lovely one. My gorgeous boy. What is it?

What's wrong?"

The confusion and terror of the first weeks of his birth came back to her. The throbbing in her bitten breast. The extended dreams, the way her anxieties seemed to spread beyond the safe fencing of her sleeping mind. Could it be happening again? She knew the answer: no. No. It was not the same. The heavy sadness was not there, the listlessness, the lack of sleep. It was not the same. And yet nothing else could explain the singing in the night, the babbling of strange babies, the shadow-baby crawling in the far corner of the room.

"I love you," she whispered, again and again, into the crook of her baby's neck. His face was turned, so that his plump cheek rested against her own, his eyes closed. Sleeping.

*

Padarn slept in his chair on the garden patio. Weeds grew between the flagstones; the heavy buzz of insects filled the air. Another heatwave. The sky, cloudless, seemed almost burdensome in its perfect blue. Elin was drinking a gin and tonic. She made it from the bottle of gin she'd found under the sink, along with whisky. Mark had bought the spirits and not mentioned it to her.

All morning Padarn had dozed, eaten happily, and slept again. At playtime, he'd had little energy or patience. She'd been the nurse again – taking his temperature, checking his little body for rashes. She found nothing. The virus made a visit to the GP impossible; besides, she hadn't got round to registering at the local surgery. Physically there was nothing wrong with her son, and so she'd decided – actively, fiercely – not to worry. She would sit and enjoy the sunshine. She would drink like everything was right in the world and she was happy. The afternoon was long, the sky was blue,

her mother and sister – miles away – loved her, and so did
her son, and so did her husband, if he thought about it
between his mania for drumming up paid work.

Elin sang, as she liked to do, to relax. It was a song
Padarn loved to hear as a four-month-old, lying in her
arms, looking up into her face:

Ar lan y môr, mae rhosys cochion
Ar lan y môr mae lilis gwynion
Ar lan y môr mae 'nghariad inne
yn cysgu'r nos a chodi'r bore

Beside the sea red roses growing
Beside the sea white lilies showing
Beside the sea their beauty telling
My true love sleeps within her dwelling

A romantic tune. The image of lovers, waking on the
beach after a night of togetherness, surrounded by flowers,
red and white. She and Mark had often walked along the
beach in those early months, carrying their shoes by their
laces, the cold waves rushing up the sand to envelop their
feet. Sometimes they walked before going to bed together.
Sometimes they walked after, the memory of his body still
on her hands, her lips, making the walk sweeter and more
intimate.

Mark was in the kitchen, putting a bowl of yesterday's
curry into the microwave for his lunch. Elin stood up as
soon as she heard the clatter of bowls, but instead of going
to him, she walked away, into the garden, still humming
the tune. The memories she had were lovely, and she didn't
want to risk having her reverie interrupted by an argument
in the kitchen. He preferred if she stayed away in the
day; she knew that without having to be told. It was like a
presence, his stress. She didn't like the word 'stress' because

it didn't seem serious or grave enough for what was ailing him.

"Hallo there!"

Elin jumped, hand on heart. It was Georgina. She was wearing an old khaki raincoat and a pink neckerchief, despite the sun.

"Lovely weather," Georgina commented. "How's the bundle of joy?"

"He's... he's fine. Great. Napping," she managed.

"Sorry to scare you the other day. Mama rightly chastised me later. Told me I shouldn't have introduced myself with a smashed rat in my hand. I'm a country girl at heart, you see."

Elin was a country girl too. She'd grown up partly on her grandparents' farm. They didn't habitually carry dead animals in their hands, but she said nothing. "Don't worry about it."

"How are you keeping with this virus business? I was saying to Mama, it makes no difference to us. We keep to ourselves anyway."

"Hm," Elin said. "Well, I suppose it's the same with us. We don't know anyone here."

"Apart from me and Mama now, isn't it?"

"Right." Elin smiled. "You'll have to come over when all this is better."

"Thanks for the offer but my mother hasn't left the house or garden since 1973. Agoraphobia. Terrible affliction."

"Oh dear. Is that... is that the fear of wide-open spaces?"

"Leaving the familiar, I'd say. She always imagines the worst."

"Like my husband," Elin went on, without realising what she was saying. "I mean, he's not phobic or anything. Just a pessimist."

"A pessimist, yes. My mother isn't a pessimist by nature, not really, but all the same she prefers to be close to home, and to me. She likes to keep an eye on me, even though I'm almost seventy now. Seventy next month."

"Oh happy birthday," Elin said, then felt stupid. "For then. For the future."

Georgina gave her a brisk smile and was about to go when Elin blurted out what she'd tried desperately not to ask: "You mentioned children..."

"Excuse me?"

"Children. A family that used to live here? You said there was a woman my age."

"That's right. Many years ago now."

"How old were the children?"

Georgina went quite still. "You want to know their ages?"

"Please. If you know." Elin glanced at the fir tree that, despite the sunny day, still threw dark shapes at the far end of the garden. She had no reason to ask. "Out of interest."

"The girl was eight. The boy around a year, if the newspapers are to be believed."

"Newspapers?"

Georgina stepped back, shaking her head, as though annoyed with herself. "Oh shoot. I didn't want to say anything. I promised Mama I wouldn't say anything."

"Say what? What happened?"

"No. I'm sorry. I just can't. I promised my mother, you see. She never went out of the house again after it happened. She blames her poorly eyes on it too because she's the one who... Well, she told me, keep schtum now about it, Georgie, otherwise you'll scare the living daylights out of them. They'll move out and then we'll never have any nice, ordinary neighbours again."

"We won't be moving out, I swear. You can tell me."

Georgina shook her head. "Sorry, dear. Shouldn't have brought it up. It's really not worth it. It doesn't change anything, knowing. Doesn't change the past, it just ruins the present."

Elin considered, for a moment, telling her about the shadow-baby, her own lullaby being sung back to her in the night. "Can you wait there for a moment? I've got something to show you."

She went back in the house to fetch the action figure from the kitchen drawer. Mark was there, scraping his leftovers into the food bin.

"It's full."

"Okay." She picked up the bin and the doll and went back outside. Georgina was nowhere to be seen. "Oh." Padarn chatted to her from his chair. "Is someone finally up now?" she asked him. He smiled at her – a wide laugh-smile that said, I see you mummy – before rubbing his ear with his hand. "Still sleepy then?"

She put the bin and toy on the ground for a moment so she could adjust his sun hat. His eyelids fluttered as sleep stole over him once again. "God," she said, because she didn't know what else to do about her son's lethargy. Then, all of a sudden, his eyes opened wide and he made a grab at the orange action figure. "Do you want this, bach?" He grabbed at it again, swiped it out of her hand, and began to violently twist its arms back and forth, banging it against the steel frame of the chair.

She watched him for a moment; his movements jerky, unfamiliar in their focus – he'd been sluggish a second ago, and now he was concentrated, intent on folding back the toy's limbs. As long as he's not crying, she thought, suppressing her unease. He's fine. Physically fine.

The compost bin was pushed up against the fence; a creeping plant grew around it, covering its plastic body. She opened the top while peering into the neighbours' garden. Georgina must have thought it better to run away than risk revealing anymore of the old inhabitants. A newspaper. So the family's ages had turned up in the newspaper. Eight and one. Why else would you note the age of children unless to record their deaths?

The conservatory doors opened and out came the old woman, Georgina's mother, doubled over a Zimmer frame. Long whisps of white hair grew down below her ears, while most of her scalp was balding, with purple and pink areas like bruises or scabs. The old woman moved to the chair surprisingly quickly, put her feet up on the upturned flowerpot again. Her eyes closed against the bright sunshine.

Elin emptied the bin into the compost when she saw, at the bottom of the foul-smelling container, a writhing beneath the half-made soil. Unwillingly, she looked closer: the earth was moving. It was not earthworms or beetles or benign insects, but a large meaty animal. A fat rat, with coarse brown fur. And beneath the rat there was a dozen pink, translucent sacks of squirming, twitching flesh. Dozens of baby rats, blindly suckling on the mother-rat's stretched teats. Elin dropped the lid, disgust rising at the back of her throat.

She stood there for a while, thinking only of Georgina's shovel: the massacred bodies of tiny rats, headless, stumps bleeding onto her lawn. Her hands trembled as she picked up the food bin; there was a strange light feeling beneath the soles of her feet, as though they were not strong enough to hold her as she walked.

What would she do with the rats? Nothing. She wasn't capable. She wouldn't tell Mark; it would only upset him.

The old woman said, "Hello. I can tell someone's there. I might be blind, but I have a good feeling about these things." Elin stopped in her tracks: the old woman's voice reminded her of a headteacher. "Is it the new neighbour?"

"Yes. Hi. Hello." Elin's voice, by contrast, sounded hesitant, scratchy. Shocked, somehow, into weakness. "I'm Elin. I'm here with my son, Padarn. He's eleven months. Almost a year now."

"Georgina told me it was a young family. That's nice, I said. How lovely." The old woman's eyes were still closed, but she was leaning forward, her head tilted. "How do you find it here?"

"Good," Elin said.

She would have to do small talk then, it seemed. They discussed the weather and the state of the garden; the changes the property developer had made to the house; the neighbours on the other side who worked at the hospital and were never at home.

"The builder had a job on his hands with this one. Georgie told me there were two skips outside, full of the old things. What colour did he paint the walls?"

"White."

"And the floors?"

"Grey carpet. Apart from the bathroom. White tiles."

"Good, good," the old woman said, as though satisfied with his work. "Good and clean. Get rid of all that rubbish."

"Especially after what happened," Elin ventured. The old woman leaned back, turned her head away slightly. "Did Georgie say something?"

"No. I read about it online."

"Oh," the old woman said, nodding. "I suppose everything is on computers now."

There was a pause; Elin, waiting for the woman to add something, to explain.

"It was a tragedy," Elin pushed.

The old woman nodded.

"I know," Elin went on, approaching the fence so that her husband might not hear. "I know this might sound odd. But at night, in the nursery... I know it sounds mad. But I think I saw the boy. The boy that used to live here. Just for a second. Do you believe in things like that? Maybe it was my imagination. It probably was..."

"It wouldn't surprise me," she said. "He was born there and he died there, too."

"How did he die?"

"I thought you knew."

"Not... not everything." She laid a hand on the fence, gripping it for balance. "I'd like to know, just in case I see him again."

"It's not a story you want to hear, love. Aren't you better off enjoying your new home without this?"

"I'll be fine," Elin said, impatiently. "I know they died. I can feel it in the night, in the nursery."

"I found the girl in the garden among the trees. The boy was upstairs. At first, I thought he'd survived. Perhaps the man had forgotten about him, I thought. But no. The police later said he'd been the first to die. The last to go was the father, of course. Hanged himself. He used a knife on his children. Revenge on the ex-wife, they said in the papers."

"You found them?"

The old woman nodded. "I heard the screams." She turned to face Elin. "It's what did for my sight. Every time I open my eyes, I see them. If I opened them now, I'd see the girl, coming to the fence to talk about her day. I'd see the boy, trying to crawl between his sister's legs. I see them, alive and dead, I see them. So it's better for me," she said, "if I don't see at all."

*

Later that day, Elin drove through a red light, clipped the curb when turning the corner into the supermarket car park. She swore and Paddy wailed on hearing his mother's tone.

"Don't cry. Don't cry. You've been sleeping all day and now you decide to wake up? Fucking hell!"

She slammed her feet down on the brake in rage. Rage at herself for not keeping calm, for driving dangerously, for putting their lives at risk because she was.... what? Frightened? Rage at her son for not behaving like an eleven-month-old should. Rage at her husband for concealing the history of the house, because, as she'd hurtled across the roundabout, she'd realised why Mark had been so enthusiastic about it in the first place; why he'd insisted on putting in an offer before she had a chance to look at it herself; why he'd discouraged her from examining the survey and housing reports too closely. He'd dealt with the lawyer. And he'd deliberately given her some pieces of information while withholding others. She knew it was true because it was so typical of him. Typical Mark to mitigate the truth, to turn something his way with storytelling and evasion. Dammit. Fuck him. Fuck him. She hit the steering wheel with the palm of her hand while Padarn cried. Fuck him for not telling me the truth.

Things didn't improve once she was inside the supermarket. She kept pushing her trolley so close to other people that a security guard had to have a word with her; she forgot essential items – the effing milk – she could not go back for it because of the new one-way system. Padarn would not stop crying. The sight of the aisles, the queues of other people, the atmosphere of suppression and panic, pushed him over the edge. Tears flowed down his cheeks and all she could think of was how baby tears were pure cortisone: they were the very chemical of stress, liquid unhappiness, dripping all down his face.

Then she had to drive home. Home to her equally unhappy husband, the crazy old woman who saw corpses whenever she opened her eyes, the rats. She was so distracted that she came close to knocking over a cyclist. Pulling into a bus stop, Elin tried to calm her nerves, her unexpected rage. For a moment, she even entertained the idea of driving back to her family in Ceredigion. She could spend lockdown in Mam's spare room. She could do the shop, look after her as best she could... But it wasn't possible. Elin could be carrying the virus without knowing, especially after that shoddy shopping trip where a security guard breathed into her face while telling her to keep her distance. No, no. It was all her fault; she was always crumbling at the slightest difficulty. She had to keep it together. For God's sake, she told herself, keep it together. A bus beeped behind her. "Shit."

*

"Where are the Nespresso capsules?" Mark asked.

She was lying on the playmat in the living room with Padarn who was, again, asleep beside her.

"Aren't there any more in the cupboard? Top shelf?"

"No."

"Oh," she said. "I forgot to get them."

Mark stood over her, an empty mug in his hand, wearing the same clothes from two days ago: a navy t-shirt with a fleck of dried gravy on the collar, black joggers. His hair was shaggy now, falling into his eyes so that he had to jerk his head to the side every five minutes, making him appear more irritable.

"I reminded you. I sent you a message."

"Yeah. I didn't see it until after. I haven't really been checking my phone today."

"What's the point of having a phone if you don't check it?"

"Sorry," she said, pushing herself onto her knees. "I'll buy them next time."

"Can't you go out now?"

"Now?" The idea terrified her. "I've just been."

"What am I supposed to drink then?"

"I don't know. There's tea, isn't there?"

"But no milk," he said. "What did you even buy? Did you actually go to the shops?"

"Yes," she said. "It was mayhem."

"I've got stuff to do," he said, waving the mug for emphasis. "I know I'm home, but I'm not home, okay? I'm working. I'm working on countless freelance projects, drumming up work to pay the bills. I've got emails flooding in, online meetings that last bloody hours. There's no way I can get it all done, which is why I'm working every day until midnight. For us. For little Padarn. So Elin, I'm asking you. Please help me. Please do the actual fucking shopping. Okay?"

She got up, drew him away from their napping baby, whispered, "Stop swearing at me. This whole week all you've been doing is swearing at me. It's not okay, Mark."

"You're not okay. What happened last night? You were acting deranged. I had to practically pin you to the floor to stop you from waking Padarn for no reason."

She bit her lip, stung. "You think you're working all the time, but why don't you try doing my job?" Elin tried hard to avoid going down this path, but now that the words had left her mouth she felt pleased, buoyed up by righteous indignation. "I get up at half five every morning, because that's when he wakes up. I feed him, clothe him, wash him, play with him, soothe him to sleep. I do the housework, the shopping, the cooking. Do you know how many times I do the laundry? Every day, Mark. I put the clothes in the machine. Take them out. Fold them. Tidy them away, and the next day I've got to do it all again. Every day the same hard work, again and again, and I don't get any rest. Not even at night, because I'm the one who gets up at all hours, anytime he needs me, and you won't let me bring him into our bed in case I might actually have a night's sleep for once!"

Mark wasn't looking at her. No, he was staring at their baby, the one who looked so much like Elin. His expression one of disdain, as though the baby was at the root of this argument, as though he should be answering for his mother's complaints, not Mark.

"Have you finished?" he asked, infuriatingly calm.

"I don't know. It depends if you listened."

"Just remember the Nespresso capsules tomorrow, okay? That's all."

Elin laughed. It came out of her in a rush. She slapped her hand over her mouth, too late to keep it in. Mark's jaw tightened. He drew back his arm and, for a second, she thought he was aiming directly at her head. She flinched, drew back, before hearing the coffee mug shattering against the wall behind her.

"Mark!"

He turned to go back into the study.

"Wait!" she shouted. "I know, Mark. I know."

He froze, one hand on the doorframe, looking away from her. "What are you talking about?"

"I know about the house, Mark. Why was it so cheap? Why did you get such a bargain?"

"What are you on about?"

"I can't believe you bought this horrible place and I can't believe you lied to me about what happened. The family that used to live here…" The word stuck in her throat; she could hardly get it out. "Murdered."

He laughed and turned to face her. "That's what this is all about? God's sake, Elin. Who cares! It's ancient history."

"Ancient! Barely twenty years ago."

"I bet you couldn't find an inch in the whole world where someone hasn't snuffed it. Look – where you're standing right there, maybe three, four, five people have died there or had their throats cut or whatever. What does it matter? It doesn't."

"It does matter…" she began.

"No surprises that you'd be hysterical about it, though. How did you find out? Actually, don't tell me. I don't care."

Mark closed the door without a word, leaving her with the fat porcelain splinters littered around her feet. "Mark!" She knocked furiously on the study door, gave it a kick. "I haven't finished!"

The door swung open and Mark's face appeared sweating and red an inch from hers. "I've finished. Now leave me the fuck alone."

The door slammed shut. She stood in the kitchen, staring at the shards on the shining white floor tiles, breathing deeply.

Why was he like this? Perhaps she'd deserved it. She knew, didn't she, that she should never laugh at him. Never make fun of him. Her mother-in-law said he'd been like that as a child, too sensitive to be mocked, his emotions running close to the surface.

She began gathering the shards, afraid that Padarn might cut himself.

*

Dinnertime brought a reconciliation. Elin fried steaks – that much she had remembered to buy – and roasted potato chips with paprika and salt. The smell enticed Mark out, and he sat, smiling ruefully at the plate in front of him.

"Thanks," he said.

It was the way he said it – sweetly, with a glance at her – that implied he was sorry for what he'd done earlier. After a relatively easy evening getting Padarn to bed (he'd turned his head and closed his eyes as soon as she'd put him down), Elin felt gracious towards her husband. She would be the one to rise above; to cope better with the crisis of a pandemic. She would show him – as she'd been showing him all along – how competent and resolutely together and sane she was.

"Tuck in," she ordered, and he did.

The food was delicious. She'd pulled back the chaos of the morning, the rats in the compost bin, the reckless drive to the shop. In the perfect cooking of the steak, the spice of the potato, she'd saved herself.

"How's work?"

"Going well," he said.

"Great." She smiled. Finally, a normal evening in their home. The kitchen clean and ordered; her son well and asleep; her husband content, talking to her as though they were married, rather than as two housemates, pitted against each other.

*

Instead of going directly to bed after dinner, Elin stayed up to watch a film. It was a film everyone she knew had seen several months ago, but she hadn't had the chance to watch herself. She watched it badly; her gaze kept sliding off the screen, either to her phone, or to the shadow on the wall behind the TV set, which was – she reassured herself – the shadow cast by the angular, 'contemporary' lampshade. People in the film kept on talking. On and on they talked, making jokes, banter. They looked great, these movie stars pretending to be ordinary people. Their physique perfect, blinding teeth, soft smiles. She couldn't follow what they were saying, but the film was meant to be good, so she sat there until the end; thinking, the good bit is probably coming up any moment now. The credits rolled. She couldn't remember anything that had happened.

Mark came out of his study to go to the bathroom upstairs. He left the light on in the study, the orange glow spilling out onto the kitchen. She got up, looked through the open door. The sofa cushions were here, piled on the floor; he was using an old road atlas as a mouse pad. The laptop was standing on its side, the fan whirring. She went in to collect the dirty glass and empty can of coke he'd evidently used as a mixer.

But then, a voice spoke to her:

"Hey, where are you?"

She froze.

"Hey sexy. Come back to me, babe. I'm ready for you."

It was coming from the computer. Calmly, she put the dirty glass and can back on the floor, turned the laptop the right way up so that she could see who was speaking. A woman was there, on the screen, wearing nothing but a strip of black rubber round her waist. She was kneeling on her bed, wherever that was, thrusting her naked breasts towards the screen. The woman did not react when Elin appeared before her. Elin stared at the nipples, the line of the vulva where every pubic hair had been removed. The woman kept on the half-moaning talk: "Babe, type anything. Tell me what you want. I'm yours to fuck. I'm ready to –"

Elin closed the tab. Fine, she thought. It was some kind of porn website. Okay. She clicked on history and there was a long list of words she had never believed Mark would type into a search engine. Painful anal crying. Brutal deep throat crying. Crying DAP. Scrolling down the history, she discovered that there was not a single website amongst them that could be described as 'work'. She scrolled and scrolled, week after week. The searches diminished, it was true, in the short time he'd been at the office; but they still came up. The same websites. From weeks ago. Months.

"What are you doing?" Mark was in the doorway. "Get away from there."

She looked up at him; he seemed to be always above her, staring down. "I was just cleaning," she heard herself say.

"Cleaning what? My laptop?" He snatched it away from

her, snapped it shut. "You can't come in here without asking."

"Why not?"

"Because it's my space. I don't walk into..." He hesitated because she did not have her own room in the house. "I don't walk into the bathroom while you're in there, do I?"

She shook her head. "I can't believe it. I can't believe you're the one angry with me after what I saw."

"What did you see?"

"A woman. Some porno sex-cam thing. Are you paying her? Are you paying her when you're telling me we don't have enough money for the mortgage?"

"I'm not paying her."

"Well, that's a lie."

"It's got nothing to do with you."

"Of course it does. I'm your wife."

"I'm allowed to look. I'm a man. It's what men do. It's normal."

"It's not normal to pay sex workers to take off their clothes for you, Mark."

"I don't pay her. It's just a film."

"No, it's not. I heard her asking for you. She was talking to the camera."

"Shut up. You don't know anything. And if I was paying for it, it's understandable, isn't it? It's not like you make much of an effort anymore."

She pushed herself to her feet. "What?"

"Forget it."

"No, go on. It's my fault. It's my fault you're looking up this filth."

"Filth! Jesus Christ, you're such a prude. So fucking Victorian."

"Shut up, Mark."

"Don't tell me to shut up."

"You haven't been working. You've been lying to me this whole time."

"Of course I've been working! Do you think I just leave my work stuff on my computer? I delete it! Company privacy!"

"Bollocks!" She threw the coke can at him. It hit his chest, bounced on the floor, dribbling black liquid. "You're a piece of shit, Mark. A piece of shit!" The can was not enough, and so she went at him, thrashing his chest and arms. "Get out! I don't ever want to see you again!"

Mark was taller and stronger than her. He simply pushed her – a sharp shove that sent her flying, hitting her head on the floor.

"Calm down," he said, pinning her down with both hands on her chest, at the bottom of her throat. "Calm the fuck down."

Her rage evaporated, replaced by a cold fear. Mark stared into her eyes, steely and concentrated, but his jaw was jutting out, and a vein on the side of his face pulsed grotesquely. She had never seen him like this before. Never. She thought of her mother-in-law. Her advice all those years ago. She hadn't been warning Elin to take care of him; she'd been warning Elin to take care of herself.

"I'm calm," she whispered, his hand still pushing down on her lungs. "Sorry. I'm sorry. Please."

Mark fell back on his heels, allowing her to sit up. A silence passed between them. "I'm tired," she said. "I'll just... I'll just go to bed."

Mark said nothing. He was looking at the space between them, brow furrowed.

"We can talk again in the morning," she said quietly. He nodded. "Okay?" She continued; she wanted to hear his voice, just once, so she could gauge his mood, make sure that the day was finally over, and she would not have a confrontation like that again. But he didn't oblige. Instead, he got to his feet and went to pour himself a drink in the kitchen. The hiss of a can and the crash of glass on the counter were deafening in the new kind of silence that lay between them.

And then came the whisper of a melody. It floated down the stairs towards her. It was her voice; the old lullaby again, *Huna blentyn ar fy mynwes…* Only Elin wasn't singing.

She ascended the stairs slowly, her hand trembling on the banister. By the time she reached the landing, the house was silent again.

*

In the old flat above the bike shop, the one within a mile of her mother and sister, the furniture was included in the rent. For years, they lived with cheap pinewood and MDF items that would regularly break. In the new house, they had brought only their second-hand sofa, the kitchen utensils, clothing. The bed was new, but because of the speed with which they'd moved, they ordered it online without ever having tested it. It irked her – the hardness of the mattress, the ugly footboard and too-low headboard; the way the bed appeared to slope downwards, so that she felt like she was slipping down a hill.

She lay there after the argument with Mark, going through things or, more accurately, letting things go through her. Waves of horrible awakening: he hadn't been working. The days he'd been locked in the study, even before the virus had made it impossible for him to go to the office, even then he'd been spending his time looking at... Talking to... Why couldn't she say it? Put it into words, she told herself. Watching porn, like all men, he'd said. Like all men. Only it wasn't, she thought, like all men. There were men who did not lie about it; men who did not replace their lives with chasing sexual gratification on a laptop screen in the dark, locked room of their first family home. Men who talked to their partners, who loved their partners

enough to be truthful. It disgusted her. Maybe she was a
prude. It disgusted her, the idea that he had been sitting on
the dining room floor, in his den, while on the other side
of the door she'd been feeding their son, carrying him in a
sling while she cooked, while she cleaned for them all, day
after day, taking the clothes out of the washing machine.
Separating the dark colours from the white.

"I can't believe it. I can't believe it."

It can't be real, she said to herself, over and over. It can't
be real. Had he really pushed her over like that? Had he
put his hand on her chest, pressing her down on the grey
carpet, so that she couldn't move? Like a warning, she
thought, to behave. Was that my husband?

Had he really typed those words into the search bar?
Words like 'brutal', 'painful'. Abbreviations she didn't
understand and did not want to understand: codewords of
violence and humiliation.

It was too late to phone her sister, despite wanting to
talk to her desperately. It was almost midnight. A message,
then? But a message would only lead to a phone call. Mark
might hear, she found herself worrying. It might upset him.
She pressed her face into the pillow, almost in tears with
the terrible knowledge that she was too frightened to speak
to her sister in case she angered her husband.

It can't be real.

She lay rigid on the bed, feet against the footboard;
the mattress like a slab of stone underneath her spine.
On their wedding day she'd worn white: a white veil, a
train long enough for her nieces to hold proudly above
their heads. The dress cost over a thousand pounds: a gift
from her parents. She began to go through the rest of the
price list: the rings, five hundred and fifty; the food and
drink, nine thousand seven hundred; the bridesmaid and
flower girl dresses, seven hundred and ten; the vintage
cars, eight hundred. Each time she remembered some

new extravagance, shame sliced through her body. That
money. She may as well have burned it. If she had burned
it, it would not have brought her the humiliation of having
married a man she could not trust. A man who wanted to
see women in pain for his sexual pleasure. Her thoughts
bounded quickly into the future – it was the end, it was
over, she would be alone, she would die alone, she would
have to raise Padarn alone, there would be lawyers, divorce
court, child support, pain, more arguments, shouting,
pushing…

And then her mind calmed, from one moment to the
next, and she retraced her steps. No, it might not happen.
We might stay together. What does it matter? He's right.
All men do it. It's normal to lie about it, to conceal…
It's a private matter. Private fantasies, even from a wife.
Everyone has their fantasies. It doesn't mean he would ever
want to do it like that in real life. It may be temporary:
the craziness of a pandemic, lack of work, the pressure of
paying bills. Fine. Temporary madness. She could forgive
temporary madness; after all, she'd experienced it herself.
It would get better, and that trajectory – the one of lawyers
and divorces and those heavy words she'd never dreamed
could apply to her – would recede into impossibility once
more.

A moment later and the woman's voice came back to
her: Babe… tell me what you want. The strip of black
material, the extreme curves of the woman's body,
the horror of hearing a stranger speaking like that to
her husband. The look her husband gave her, full of
condescension. Frigid, he called her, because she was not
part of that world.

She was arguing with herself – he is a pig; all men do it;
all men are pigs; I should forgive him; I will not forgive him
– when all her thoughts were flattened by shrieking coming
from the direction of the nursery. It was a cry that sounded

like Padarn's throat was raw with crying. It was dry and miserable and desperate, as though he'd been crying for a long time. She went to him, opened the nursery door, flicked on the switch.

The lightbulb flashed once then died. Padarn stopped crying.

Elin fumbled around for her phone in the back of her pocket, saying 'sh' all the time. In the background she heard her 'sh' come back to her. "Sh," she said. "Sh," came the echo. Someone in the room who was making fun of her. In the beam of her phone light, she saw it again – the shadow-baby. The one who had crawled away into the corner of the room. He was standing against her son's cot. One hand was reaching inside, offering her son the orange toy she'd discovered in the garden. Her son reached for it.

"No," she said. "Don't touch it."

The shadow-baby turned to face her. It seemed to sway slightly, still unsure of its balance, head right back, so that its bruises were illuminated by the light: the blue turning into black, its eyes full of blood, as though they'd been crushed.

"Give it to me," she said, holding out her hand.

"No," said the shadow-baby in her voice.

"Then leave," she said. "You don't live here anymore."

"No," said her voice from the too-red lips of the child.

"You've been stealing," she said, hurriedly. "You've stolen something from Padarn. He's not been himself. Give it back, whatever you've got. Give it to me."

"Give it to me," he said. "Give it."

"What do you want?"

"Stolen," he said.

"What is it? What did you steal?"

The shadow-baby lost its balance, crumpled onto the floor; all the while, its bloodshot eyes were fixed on her. He began to cry, but the cries were not the cries of a baby.

They were an adult's cries, a grown woman. Like her cries. She put her hands over her mouth. He was crying with her voice… Then, suddenly, the sobs became a growl, threatening and low, as though, like a dog, he'd seen something he didn't like.

"What are you doing?"

A tug from behind her. Cold flesh on her wrists from where her husband grabbed her.

"Look," she said, pointing at the snarling visitor. "He's upset."

"He's not crying."

"Look," she said.

"At what? Who were you talking to?"

She paused. The baby, growling, babbling, gurgling. "You can't see him?"

"Padarn? Yes, I can see him. He's fine. Awake but fine. Why are you here? Are you deliberately waking him up?"

"No," she said. "I wasn't the one who woke him."

Mark's hand gripped her arm tightly. "Tell me what you can see, Elin," he said calmly.

A pause. The shadow-baby grinned, let out a laugh that sounded more like a groan, and as it laughed it tipped its little head back. Back and back until it hung down its shoulderblades and she could see into the deep red flesh of its neck.

"Nothing," she whispered, forcing herself to speak even though her whole body was shaking. Mark can't find out. It was the only thing that was keeping her from fainting.

"I don't believe you. I heard you talking. You were having a conversation with someone who isn't there."

The baby continued to growl, clinging onto the side of the cot, trying to pull itself up on its feet.

"No," she said, forming the words slowly. "Just with myself."

He shook his head. "I've been observing you these past few days. You're not well."

"I'm fine. I'm well."

"No," he said. "It's not safe for you. It's not safe for Padarn either, having you in the same room with him in the middle of the night like this. You're not yourself."

"What do you think I'm going to do?"

"Last time I found you with him in the bedroom, remember? You were standing in the dark with him in front of an open window. You were going to throw him out, remember?"

She shook her head. "I would never have done that."

"I phoned the doctors. They agreed with me."

"The window was open," she conceded slowly. "Because it was hot."

"It was January."

She bit her lip. The shadow-baby righted himself; slowly, he made his way towards them by cruising along the cot. "He's coming," she said.

"Who is?"

"He wants to steal from us," she said quietly. "He wants to steal our son from us." The child was reaching towards them, offering the orange toy, shaking it. His face a mask of bruises and crushed flesh.

Instinctively, Elin stretched out her hand to the shadow-baby, ready to take the toy from him.

"What are you doing?" he asked, staring at her outstretched arm.

The shadow-baby was close; the dank smell again, like wet clothes and old nappies. She could feel both her son and her husband watching her as she spoke to it: "Here. Let me fix it for you.'

Mark pulled her away suddenly, half-dragging her across the landing.

"Stop it!" she cried. "Let go of me!"

He pushed her into the bathroom: a kick that sent her sprawling across the tiles, her head hitting the toilet bowl. She groaned, tried to lift herself up, but by that time he'd locked the door.

"Mark!" she shouted. "Mark!"

"This is for your own safety, Elin," he said. "Stay there while I make some calls."

"No!"

"You need to see someone. You need help."

She screamed and punched the door. His footsteps receded along the corridor, down the stairs. He was not even going to check on their baby. Their baby alone with that thing. "Mark! Padarn! Get Padarn! He's not safe! Mark!"

She could hear him on the phone, using his controlled voice, his public-facing voice. Hello this is Mark Griffiths. Sorry to bother you but my wife is acting very strangely. I think she's a danger to herself and others... She continued to bang on the door and scream Padarn's name, until she heard him say "Listen to this!" and realised he was holding the phone up so that the nurse or social worker or whoever it was could hear her. She went quiet.

Padarn. She was shaking in silent panic.

The bathroom window overlooked the back garden. Beneath it was the drainpipe and then the gleam of the white fence on her left. She opened the window and studied the path: a shimmy to the left, a metre or so down the drainpipe, and then she could step onto the fence and lower herself down. There was a high probability that she would fall. But she might not. She didn't know what to do.

Then something happened that made up her mind: she saw the girl.

It was dark, but the neighbours' garden light threw a thin half-beam across the centre of the garden. Enough light for Elin to see a figure between the fir trees. She was so pale:

a streak of white among the murky branches. The girl was holding something in her hand and looking – not at Elin – but at the back door of the house. There emerged the shadow-baby, moving in its strange furtive away across the rough earth towards the trees. It half-rolled, half-crawled, its head lolling from side to side, until it reached the girl. It pressed its bruised face into her legs.

The girl looked up at Elin. She lifted a hand in the air, the one holding a knife, and pointed it at the white fence. Then they disappeared into the trees.

Stolen. The word echoed in her head. The shadow-baby was a thief, creeping into Padarn's cot at night, stealing whatever the dead can take from the living. She had to go down there; she had to go into the dark trees to take back what belonged to her and Padarn.

The girl had gestured at the fence, as though pointing the way. Elin pushed her head and shoulders as far as she could out of the bathroom window. It was possible to use the bend in the drainpipe as a step to the next windowsill, and then slip down the fence. In the background she could hear Mark on the phone. His voice rang loudly – my wife, he kept on saying, and each time he said those words she inched further out of the window. My wife needs urgent help. She's intent on hurting herself and the baby.

Yet it was him who left Padarn alone when he was crying, screaming for help…

Elin pulled back, reversed, so that she sat on the bathroom window, her legs dangling from the second floor. Slowly, she lowered herself, sticking her foot out in search of the pipe. When she found it, she placed her right sole on it and pushed down, testing if it could hold her weight. It moved easily. It couldn't possibly hold her. If she fell, she might die or, if she was lucky, break her legs and ankles. The fir trees shook slightly in the breeze. There were voices on the wind, voices that called to her, Come now. Come find us.

Padarn started to scream again.

Already she was scrambling down the drainpipe towards the fence. The bend held for the moment she needed it to hold, then crumpled. There was blood on her hands from scraping against the pebbledash wall. Elin stepped onto the white fence and jumped down onto the earth.

She froze on all fours, her feet and wrists aching from the fall. It wasn't clear from which direction the screams were coming. All around her were Padarn's cries, crashing down from the open window, sweeping over from the trees. The wailing was overwhelming, full of the pain of abandonment.

No – it was from the end of the garden. The screams came from the far end of the garden.

"Padarn!"

Elin ran to the firs, desperate for Padarn; desperate for the noise to stop. She slipped in between the branches at the same point where the girl had been. The branches enveloped her – that familiar smell, dank and rotting, made it difficult to breathe. She walked further between the trees, until the faint beam of light from the neighbours' garden was extinguished, and the world of houses and streets with it. Padarn's cries curdled into breathy sobs; he was close now – spluttering into her ear. His ragged breath against her cheek.

Underfoot, the pine-covered earth was uneven; the ground creaked and splintered under her step until her toe caught something soft. She bent down blindly, hand outstretched. Something shot out of the darkness and gripped her arm. It was Elin's turn to scream. The hold on her was dry, hard, cold – non-human. It dug down into her flesh to the bone. Elin pulled away, but the grip tightened. She kicked and hit out in all directions. "Get off me!"

She felt a searing pain across her palm. The grip

loosened and she staggered backwards, towards the light. Her hand was bleeding front and back, her fingertips raw from the wall. The flesh on the back of her hand cut open. The light caught an object at her feet – a long knife, brown with mud and pine needles, sticky with blood.

"Elin!"

She looked up: her husband was illuminated in the bathroom window, the phone glued to his ear. His face was twisted in anger – "What the fuck, Elin!" Her Padarn was still crying, but his cries now came unmistakably from the house. Why was Mark shouting at her when their baby was in distress in the next room? She went back into the house, blood dripping from her hand.

Mark was waiting for her at the top of the stairs.

She would go upstairs as calmly as possible; she would simply ask him to let her see her son. "I want to go to Padarn," she said softly when she reached him.

"You're bleeding."

"It's nothing. Mark – move out of the way. Please."

"Did you do that to yourself?" She shook her head. "Fucking hell. Is that a knife?"

She looked down at her bleeding hand. There it was: the long knife. She'd picked it up without noticing. "Give it to me," said Mark.

Padarn's cries grew more intense; his voice was raw with sobs, as though he might choke to death on his tears. "I'll give it to you if you let me pass."

He snatched the knife; she let him take it. But as she tried to move down the landing, he continued to block her path. "Mark, please."

Mark swore, threw his phone on the floor in a sudden wave of rage. "For fuck's sake, Elin! Just do what I say for once."

"I always do what you say."

"You're fucking psycho. You're mental. You need to be

locked up." He pointed the knife at her: "Get back to the bathroom, Elin."

Padarn howled. "No!" She lunged at him, trying to beat her way past, but he simply stepped forward. It seemed, for a moment, that he'd stepped into her. But that was impossible. They were so close, she could taste the sweat from his cheek, feel the anger swelling up in his chest. Then she felt it: the wrongness of something between her ribs, the crack of bone. They parted. She looked down and saw the knife; she looked up and saw Mark's expression of horror.

"Mark, why wouldn't you just let me go to him?"

He said nothing. The look of horror wasn't for Elin: his eyes were fixed behind her. On the thing that emerged from the bathroom and the open window. She turned to them: the girl and the half-crawling baby. Red slashes covered their small throats like scarves. She carried herself to the nursery, picked up her crying Padarn from the cot with the knife still inside her. He calmed as soon as she held him, quickly covering him in blood. With her baby close, she stumbled out to the landing in search of the phone but didn't make it far. She sank to the floor with him, pressing his hot, tear-stained face against her own.

Mark stood with his back to her, facing the staircase. The girl and the boy were close; they sang under their breath – Huna blentyn, huna blentyn. The smell again, although she didn't mind it as much as she used to. She buried her nose into Padarn's neck, his soft curls, so she only heard Mark's high, sharp scream, followed by the thundering of his body against the staircase. When she looked up, Mark's body was slumped at the bottom of the stairs, his neck at a right-angle. He was looking directly up at her, even though he was lying on his front.

Padarn's breath was easing; he cooed into her ear like he used to do. He said "Ma-mi, Ma-mi" with his face close to hers. "Pa-darn," she whispered back.

The other two joined them. The baby put his bruised head on her lap; the girl put her bony temple on her shoulder. From afar, the sound of the sirens drifted towards them, as Elin sang in her own voice:

Huna blentyn ar fy mynwes
Clyd a chynnes ydyw hon
Breichiau mam sy'n dynn amdanat
Cariad mam sy dan fy mron

ACKNOWLEDGEMENTS

*

All my gratitude to Rebecca Parfitt and Rhys Owain Williams for their editorial sharpness, patience, and kind encouragement. Thank you, too, to the lovely Emma Butler-Way for her meticulous reading of my drafts, and her ever-wise suggestions. Lastly, muito obrigada to Renato, who always reassured me that there was nothing to be afraid of when entering the nursery in the dead of night...

ABOUT THE AUTHOR

*

Eluned Gramich is a writer and translator from west Wales. Her memoir of her time in Hokkaido, Japan, *Woman Who Brings the Rain,* won the inaugural New Welsh Writing Awards in 2015 and went on to be shortlisted for the Wales Book of the Year in 2016. Her work has appeared in anthologies and magazines, including *Stand, Planet, New Welsh Review, The Lonely Crowd, Wales Arts Review,* and on *BBC Radio 4.* Her most recent essay is included in the anthology *Women on Nature* (Unbound Books). She lives in Cardiff with her husband and energetic toddler.

Lightning Source UK Ltd.
Milton Keynes UK
UKHW041122091121
393635UK00003B/592